Crocodile's Masterpiece

Farrar, Straus and Giroux • New York

Crocodile was a great artist. He worked hard and painted a picture every day. But nobody ever came to his studio to buy anything.

Elephant lived next door. He loved his house,
although he felt something was missing. It needed a
nice picture on the wall to make it really cozy.

"I'll go visit my neighbor, the artist," said Elephant. "Maybe he can help me." So he went over to Crocodile's house and knocked on the door.

"Hello," said Crocodile. "What can I do for you?"

"I'd like to buy a picture," said Elephant. "My house looks too bare."

Crocodile was delighted. He flung his paintbrush in the corner and brought out his paintings.

Elephant found them all so beautiful that he couldn't decide which to buy.

"I've got an idea," said Crocodile. "I'll paint something really special for you—a picture of everything you could want to see! Come back next week."

Elephant rushed home, excited. He soon discovered that a week goes very slowly when you're waiting for something. So he painted his house.

He tended his garden.

Then he reread last week's papers. Finally, the day came for Elephant to pick up his new painting.

Crocodile greeted him warmly. It was obvious that he'd been working hard. Tubes of paint and brushes were strewn everywhere, and his smock was daubed with colors. With a smile, Crocodile picked up a picture and turned it toward Elephant.

"Here it is!" he said proudly.

"But, Croc!" cried Elephant. "There's nothing on
it. It's blank!"

"It looks blank," said Crocodile quietly, "but close
your eyes and think of a picture."

"A snow scene," said Elephant, and he closed his eyes. To his surprise, a magnificent winter landscape appeared, just like one he'd seen on a Christmas card. "Fantastic!" he cried. "I'll take it."
He paid and rushed off home.

Elephant carefully hung the picture on the wall and sat down opposite it in his armchair. Then he made himself comfortable and closed his eyes.

First, a Dutch windmill appeared, with white clouds in the sky, exactly as he'd wished.

Next, there was a tropical scene with blue mountains and a sunset.

Then a rider on a horse appeared. Elephant himself was holding the reins. He spurred the horse on and galloped through the night.

The picture kept changing.
Crocodile was absolutely right, thought Elephant.
It's a masterpiece!
So the days passed and Elephant hardly stirred from his chair. His garden fell into neglect.

One night it was very hot and Elephant couldn't get
to sleep. He tossed and turned in bed.

It's a pity my masterpiece isn't in my bedroom—
then I could be enjoying my snowscape now, he
thought. But when he closed his eyes, the little village
in the white mountains appeared very clearly.
Snowflakes were swirling in a gray sky.

Elephant jumped out of bed. "What's happening?"
he cried in surprise.

He closed his eyes again and again. Each time, whatever he wished for appeared, no matter where he was—in the kitchen or in the hall. All the time the picture was still hanging in the sitting room.

Early the next morning, Elephant went back to his
neighbor.

"Croc," he said angrily, "you've cheated me! I want
a real picture!"

"You can exchange it," said Crocodile, who wasn't
the least bit upset. "Just choose whichever one you
want."

Once again, Elephant couldn't make up his mind. A sunset, a ship at sea, a still life with fruit. They were all so beautiful!

But there was no other picture with so much going
on in it as the masterpiece.

"What did I tell you?" said Crocodile. "It's a very
special work."

"Yes, you're right," answered Elephant. "Now I
understand the real beauty of your masterpiece."

He took the white canvas under his arm and hurried home.

Content, he sat down in his armchair and lived
happily ever after.

And Crocodile? He painted a lot more of those
extraordinary white pictures. Now he is famous all
over the world, and his work can be admired in
museums everywhere.